This book belongs to:

SCOOBY-DOO!

Sea Monster Scare

By Gail Herman

Illustrated by Duendes del Sur

ADVANCE PUBLISHERS

Find These Fun Activities Inside!

Check the inside back cover for fun things to do!

Bonus story-related activity strips throughout the 15 volumes.

Create your own mystery book, *Scooby-Doo The Swamp Witch!* Color, collect, and staple the coloring pages at the end of the first 12 books in the Scooby-Doo Read & Solve mystery series.

www.advancepublishers.com
Produced by Judy O Productions, Inc.
Designed by SunDried Penguin Design
All rights reserved.
Printed in China

was a perfect day for the beach.

Ret's ro!" Scooby-Doo said to his friends.

Scoob is right," Shaggy said. "Surf's up!"

COUNTING MYSTERY

How many umbrellas are in this book?

Velma pulled a wagon. It was filled with shovels and pails and flags. "I'm ready to make a one-of-a-kind sand castle!" she said.

Scooby pulled another wagon. It was filled with sandwiches and pizza, hot dogs, and tons of chips.

"We're ready for a one-of-a-kind lunch!" Shaggy said.

"This is a good spot!" said Velma. She took everything from the wagon. Then she filled the pails with sand. Fred turned them over. And Daphne lifted them up.

"This sand castle will be perfect!" said Velma.

"Mmm-mmm! This sandwich is perfect," said Shaggy.

7

Scooby and Shaggy ate their way through piles of food.
Finally, they burped.

"Like, we're all done!" said Shaggy.

"Us too," said Velma.

Shaggy and Scooby looked over. Their
jaws dropped. "Holy cow!" said Shaggy.
The castle had moats and bridges, and
winding steps. Flags flew from towers.

"It is good," Velma agreed.

"Like, I'm not talking about the castle,"
said Shaggy. "We're out of food!"

SEEK & FIND

Find the blue shovel on this page, and then four more on the following pages.

"Out of food?" Daphne laughed.

"And we didn't have a bite!" said Fred.

Scooby hung his head. "Rorry."

"Sorry," Shaggy echoed. "How about Scoob and I make a food run? There's a Snack Shack down the beach!"

Answer: one on page 13, two on page 16, one on page 29

Scooby and Shaggy set off. A little while later, they were back. At least, they thought they were. They saw the blanket. They saw Velma's book. But that was all.

"Zoinks!" said Shaggy. "Everyone has disappeared! And so has the sand castle!"

All around them, people snatched up
blankets. They threw books, bottles of
sunscreen, and other things into beach bags.
They rushed away.

"Something horrible has happened!" cried Shaggy.
"We need clues!"

13

Scooby gazed out to sea. "Rook!" he gasped. A giant sea serpent rode the waves.

"Like, that thing did it!" said Shaggy. "It took the sand castle, *and* the gang!"

Shouts rang out across the water.

"It's getting closer!" Shaggy cried.

Scooby yelped, "Run, Raggy!"

15

The buddies took off. They jumped over people. They scooted around umbrellas. But the sea serpent was close behind.

It was coming onto the beach!

"A surfboard, Scoob!" Shaggy shouted. "Quick! Hop on!"

A moment later, they bounced along the waves. "Like, hang ten, Scoob!" Shaggy said.

But they couldn't surf fast enough. The monster was closing in!

The sea grew rough. Scooby
and Shaggy hung on. Wave after
wave. Up, down. Up, down.

Scooby turned green. "Don't lose
your lunch, good buddy," Shaggy said.
Up, down. Up, down.
Shaggy turned green too.

All at once, a giant wave crashed over them.
Shaggy clung to Scooby. Scooby clung to Shaggy.
Whoosh!

Find the differences between Shaggy on this page and the one below.

Up, up, up they went. The surfboard went one way. Scooby and Shaggy went the other way.

Answer: missing green strip in surfboard, shirt is yellow.

They hung in the air. Then they dropped — fast. Right onto the back f the sea serpent!

"Help!" "Relp!" they cried.

"Don't worry," said Velma. "We're right here."

Scooby spun around. Velma, Fred, and Daphne were on the serpent's back, too.

"Ride?" said Shaggy. "The serpent gives rides?"

"It's not a real monster," said Daphne. "It's a float."

Scooby and Shaggy gazed around. People were laughing and having fun.

"But what about the people on the beach?" asked Shaggy.
"Why did they run away? And what about the sand castle?
I thought a monster wiped it out."

"The sand castle is gone?" Velma gasped.

29

Then she sighed. "It must have been the tide. That's what happens with sand castles. The tide sweeps them away. And those people? They were only moving away from the water."

The monster float stopped with a bump.
They were back at their spot at the beach.
"Like, forget the sand castle," said Shaggy.
"All our food has been swept away, too!"

MYSTERY MIX-UP

Unscramble the letters
to solve these
word mysteries.

cbahe

bsfodraur

vawe

ase psretne

otlfa

"Rack Rack?" said Scooby.
"Snack Shack!" agreed Shaggy.
Scooby-Dooby Doo!

Create your
own bonus
book!

Step 1:
Color both sides of
this storybook page.

Step 2:
With an adult's
supervision, carefully
cut along the dotted
line.

Step 3:
Repeat steps 1 and 2
for the first 12 books of
the Scooby-Doo Read
& Solve mystery series.

Please turn page over for
further instructions.

It was Zeke and Zeb!

"I gotta hand it to you kids," said the sheriff, "for finding that hijacked armored car."

"These two goons hid it in the swamp," said Fred.

"And dressed up like a witch and zombie to protect their loot," added Velma.

"Time to go home—and eat!" said Shaggy.

Slurp! "Rooby-Rooby-Roo!" agreed Scoob.

24

Step 4:
Put all 12 cut-out page neatly in order.

Step 5:
Staple three times on the left side of the paper stack to create the book's spine.

Step 6:
Congratulations, you have solved the mystery!

You have now created your very own Scooby-Doo storybook!